DRIVE AND FIND!

 phoenix international publications, inc.

Blaze and his best friend, AJ, live in Axle City—an awesome place filled with races, chases, and mighty Monster Machines! Search this city scene for Blaze and his pals:

AJ

Blaze

Zeg

Darington

Gabby

Stripes

Starla

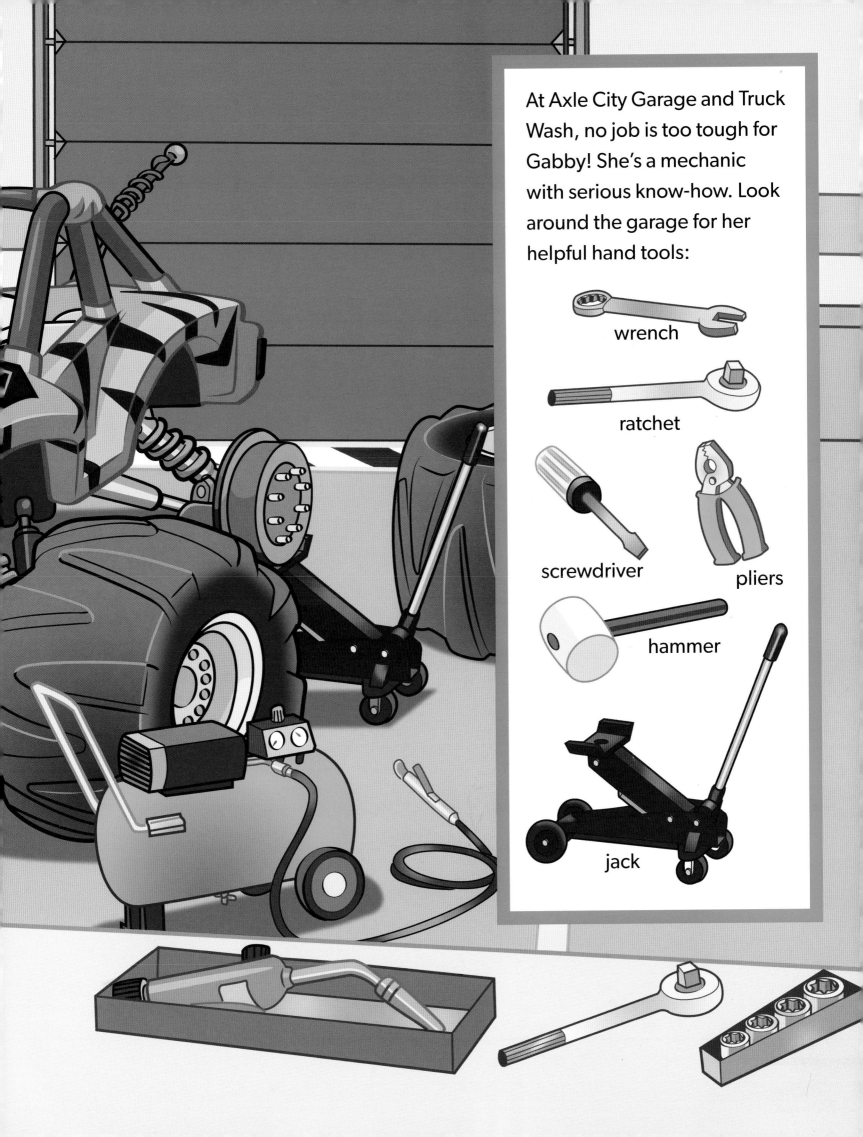

At Axle City Garage and Truck Wash, no job is too tough for Gabby! She's a mechanic with serious know-how. Look around the garage for her helpful hand tools:

wrench

ratchet

screwdriver

pliers

hammer

jack

Beep-beep! Smash! Thud!
Blaze and Zeg are using FORCE to help knock over things at a busy construction site. Look for their construction vehicle friends:

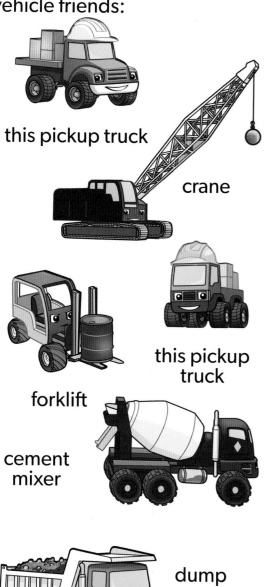

this pickup truck

crane

forklift

this pickup truck

cement mixer

dump truck

Let's Blaaaze! Blaze, Darington, Crusher, and Pickle head to the Badlands on the outskirts of Axle City for a Team Truck Challenge race. As the Monster Machines ACCELERATE around the racecourse, can you find two flags of each color?

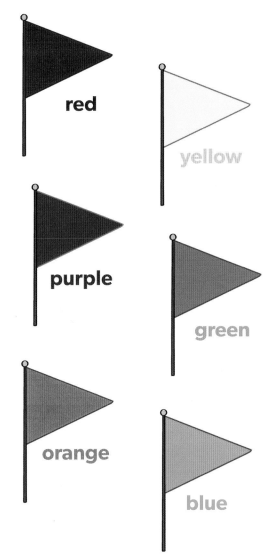

red

yellow

purple

green

orange

blue

Roar! It's time to play hide-and-seek in Stripes's jungle home! Can you find Stripes, Blaze, and these other friends who are hiding?

AJ

Stripes

Blaze

Gabby

Zeg

Starla

Anchors aweigh! Sometimes the Monster Machines race on water, too! As Blaze and AJ sail past Crusher and Pickle, help them look around for these ocean-themed things:

buoy

life jacket

bubbles

robot shark

this island

this sail

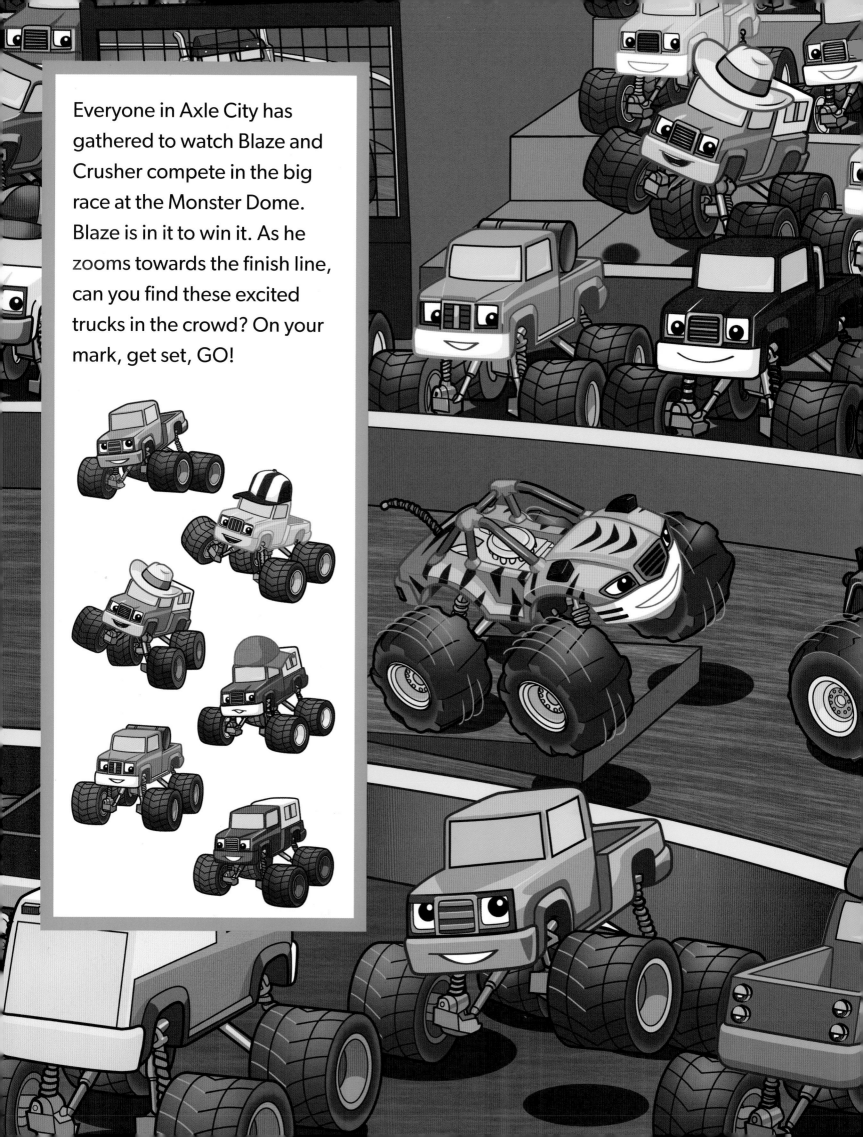

Everyone in Axle City has gathered to watch Blaze and Crusher compete in the big race at the Monster Dome. Blaze is in it to win it. As he zooms towards the finish line, can you find these excited trucks in the crowd? On your mark, get set, GO!

What's ifferent?

Yeehaw! **Starla and Blaze are showing off their skills.**

Answers on the next page!

Throw it in reverse and head back to Axle City to see what you can find:

- **above** the Monster Dome

- **below** the sun

- **in front of** the Monster Dome

- **next to** Crusher

- **behind** Gabby

- **on** Starla's head

The **sun** is located in outer space, and **clouds** are located in Earth's atmosphere. Which do you think is closer to the Monster Dome, the sun or the clouds?

Answers: cloud, tree, Crusher, Pickle, spare tires, a hat

Go back to Axle City Garage and search for these other cool tools:

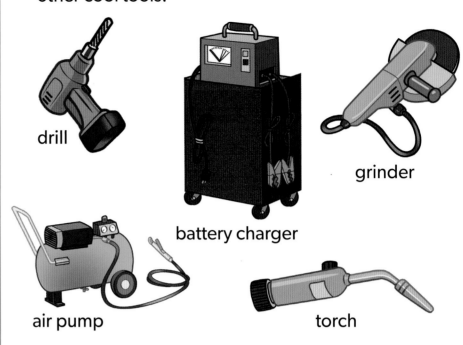

drill

battery charger

grinder

air pump

torch

An **air pump** is a tool that pumps air into something. Which part of Stripes needs air?

Cruise back to the construction site and find these shapes:

- square
- triangle
- rectangle
- oval
- circle
- diamond

Do you think a **circle** is the best shape for a wheel? Why?

Drive back to the Badlands to find things that rhyme with these words:

- tree
- maze
- steel
- zoom
- fun
- car

What other words can you think of that rhyme with the words in this list?

Answers: bee, fume, Blaze, sun, wheel, star

Journey back to the jungle to find and count these things:

- **1** slide
- **2** clouds
- **3** rocks
- **4** flowers
- **5** shrubs
- **6** palm trees

Which **rock** do you think is the **heaviest**? Why?

Water begins with **w**. **W**ade back to the ocean and find these other things that also begin with the letter **w**:

- **w**aves
- **w**hale
- **w**ind
- **w**heel
- **w**ing

Buoyancy is the ability of something to float in water. Which do you think is more **buoyant**, a **whale** or a **wrench**?

Blaze back to the Monster Dome and find these car parts:

- tire
- taillight
- hood
- headlights
- bumper
- windshield

Who do you think is going to win the race?

"What's Different?" Answer Key